FLEXI VIOLIN 2

Paul Harris and Jessica O'Leary

VIOLIN (SOLO AND ACCOMPANIMENT) PART

ff FABER MUSIC

INTRODUCTION

The FLEXI VIOLIN series brings together a diverse range of enjoyable and colourful pieces for the developing violinist to study and perform. We've chosen the title Flexi because the pieces can be performed in a number of different ways: violin with piano accompaniment, violin duet (with the teacher or more advanced student playing the second part) or two violins and piano accompaniment. Every combination provides a complete and satisfying performance.

Jessica O'Leary and Paul Harris

© 2022 by Faber Music Ltd
This edition first published in 2022
Bloomsbury House, 74–77 Great Russell Street, London WC1B 3DA
Music processed by Jackie Leigh
Cover design by Chloë Alexander Design
Printed in England by Caligraving Ltd
All rights reserved

ISBN10: 0-571-54270-0
EAN13: 978-0-571-54270-3

To buy Faber Music publications or to find out about the full range of titles available please contact your local music retailer or Faber Music sales enquiries:

Faber Music Ltd, Burnt Mill, Elizabeth Way, Harlow CM20 2HX
Tel: +44 (0) 1279 82 89 82
fabermusic.com

CONTENTS

	Duet part	Solo part
Far Awa' Amy Beach	4	5
The Last Rose of Summer Irish traditional	6	7
Air de ballet Cécile Chaminade	8	9
To a Wild Rose Edward MacDowell	10	11
Deep River Samuel Coleridge-Taylor	12	13
The Seasons Antonio Vivaldi	14	15
Air from Orchestral Suite No.3 J.S. Bach	16	17
Gavotte Cécile Chaminade	18	19
Presto Op. 99 Joseph Haydn	20	21
Yo te adoro Francisca Gonzaga	22	23
Catherine the Storyteller Paul Harris	24	25
Duetto No. 2 Franz Krommer	26	27
Duo principale Joseph Bologne	28	29
Slavic March Cécile Chaminade	32	33
Sonata No. 4 George Frideric Handel	34	35

Violin accompaniment

Far Awa' (duet part)

Amy Beach
(1867–1944)

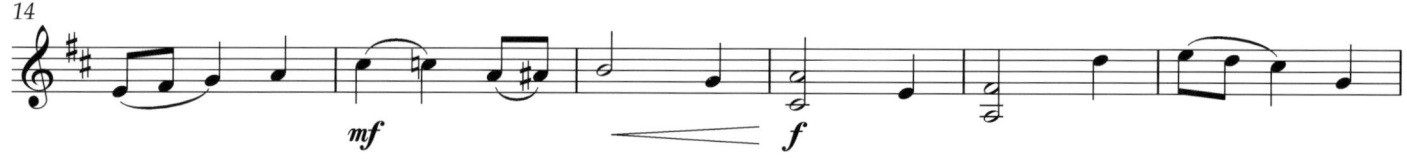
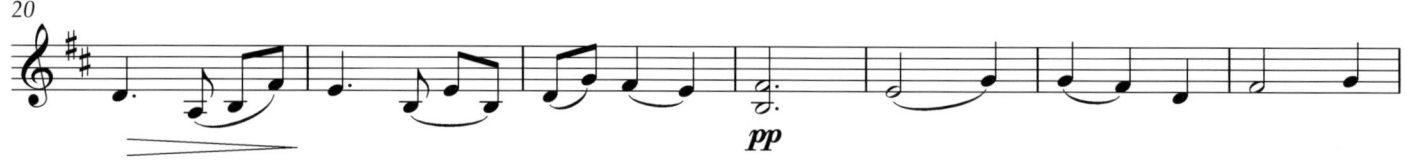

© 2022 by Faber Music Ltd.

Violin solo

Far Awa'

Amy Beach
(1867–1944)

Violin accompaniment

The Last Rose of Summer (duet part)

Irish traditional

© 2022 by Faber Music Ltd.

Violin solo

The Last Rose of Summer

Irish traditional

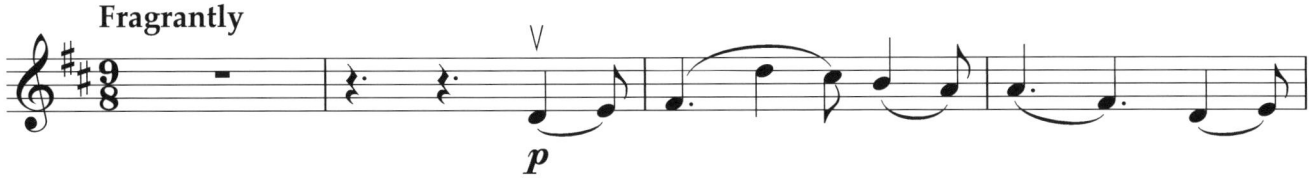

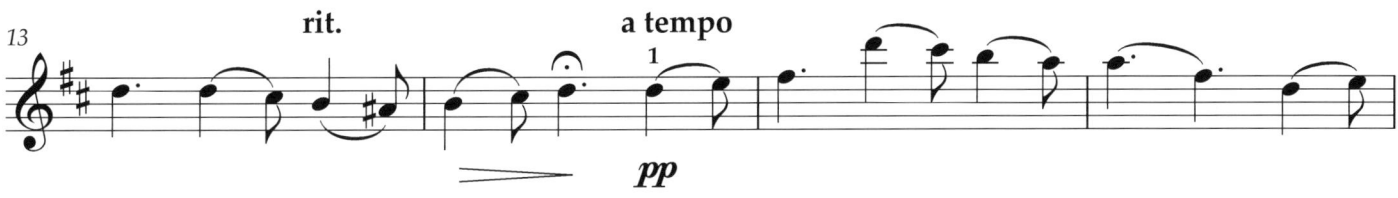
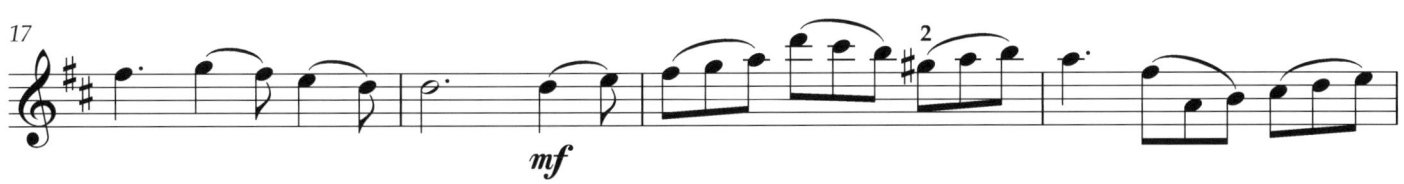

© 2022 by Faber Music Ltd.

Violin accompaniment

Air de ballet (duet part)

Cécile Chaminade
(1857–1944)

© 2022 by Faber Music Ltd.

Air de ballet

Violin solo

Cécile Chaminade
(1857–1944)

To a Wild Rose (duet part)

Edward MacDowell
(1860–1908)

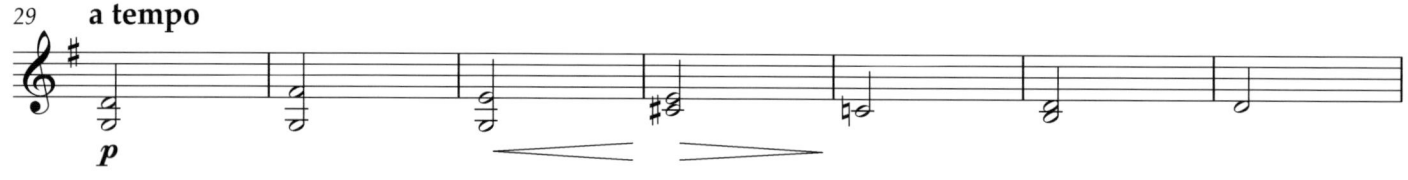
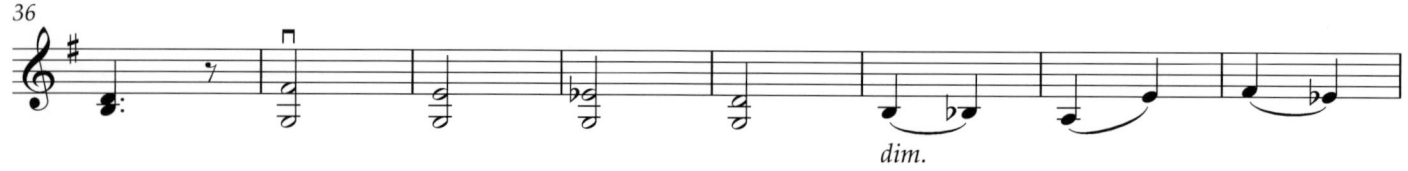

© 2022 by Faber Music Ltd.

To a Wild Rose

Edward MacDowell
(1860–1908)

Violin accompaniment

Deep River (duet part)

Samuel Coleridge-Taylor
(1875–1912)

© 2022 by Faber Music Ltd.

Violin solo

Deep River

Samuel Coleridge-Taylor
(1875–1912)

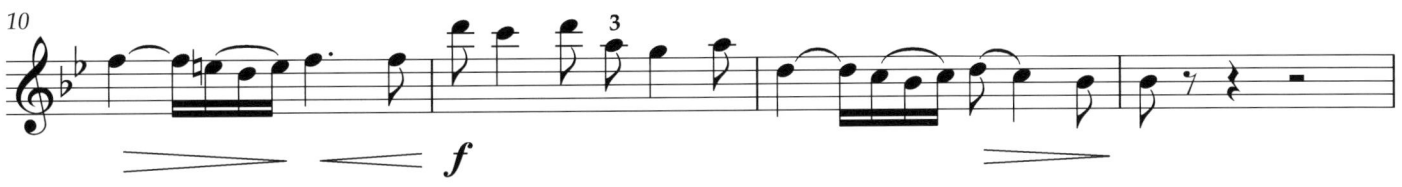

© 2022 by Faber Music Ltd.

The Seasons (duet part)

Antonio Vivaldi
(1678–1741)

Violin solo

The Seasons

Antonio Vivaldi
(1678–1741)

Violin accompaniment

Air from Orchestral Suite No. 3 (duet part)

Johann Sebastian Bach
(1685–1750)

© 2022 by Faber Music Ltd.

Violin solo

Air from Orchestral Suite No. 3

Johann Sebastian Bach
(1685–1750)

Violin accompaniment

Gavotte (duet part)

Cécile Chaminade
(1857–1944)

FLEXI VIOLIN 2

Paul Harris and Jessica O'Leary

PIANO ACCOMPANIMENT

ff FABER MUSIC

INTRODUCTION

The FLEXI VIOLIN series brings together a diverse range of enjoyable and colourful pieces for the developing violinist to study and perform. We've chosen the title Flexi because the pieces can be performed in a number of different ways: violin with piano accompaniment, violin duet (with the teacher or more advanced student playing the second part) or two violins and piano accompaniment. Every combination provides a complete and satisfying performance.

Jessica O'Leary and Paul Harris

© 2022 by Faber Music Ltd
This edition first published in 2022
Bloomsbury House, 74–77 Great Russell Street, London WC1B 3DA
Music processed by Jackie Leigh
Cover design by Chloë Alexander Design
Printed in England by Caligraving Ltd
All rights reserved

ISBN10: 0-571-54270-0
EAN13: 978-0-571-54270-3

To buy Faber Music publications or to find out about the full range of titles available please contact your local music retailer or Faber Music sales enquiries:

Faber Music Ltd, Burnt Mill, Elizabeth Way, Harlow CM20 2HX
Tel: +44 (0) 1279 82 89 82
fabermusic.com

CONTENTS

Far Awa' Amy Beach 4

The Last Rose of Summer Irish traditional 6

Air de ballet Cécile Chaminade 8

To a Wild Rose Edward MacDowell 10

Deep River Samuel Coleridge-Taylor 12

The Seasons Antonio Vivaldi 14

Air from Orchestral Suite No.3 J.S. Bach 17

Gavotte Cécile Chaminade 20

Presto Op. 99 Joseph Haydn 23

Yo te adoro Francisca Gonzaga 26

Catherine the Storyteller Paul Harris 29

Duetto No. 2 Franz Krommer 32

Duo principale Joseph Bologne 36

Slavic March Cécile Chaminade 43

Sonata No. 4 George Frideric Handel 46

Far Awa'

Amy Beach
(1867–1944)

The Last Rose of Summer

Irish traditional

Air de ballet

Cécile Chaminade
(1857–1944)

© 2022 by Faber Music Ltd.

To a Wild Rose

Edward MacDowell
(1860–1908)

© 2022 by Faber Music Ltd.

11

Deep River

Samuel Coleridge-Taylor
(1875–1912)

© 2022 by Faber Music Ltd.

The Seasons

Antonio Vivaldi
(1678–1741)

Air from Orchestral Suite No. 3

Johann Sebastian Bach
(1685–1750)

Gavotte

Cécile Chaminade
(1857–1944)

© 2022 by Faber Music Ltd.

Presto Op. 99

Joseph Haydn
(1732–1809)

© 2022 by Faber Music Ltd.

Yo te adoro

Francisca Gonzaga
(1847–1935)

© 2022 by Faber Music Ltd.

Catherine the Storyteller

Paul Harris

© 2022 by Faber Music Ltd.

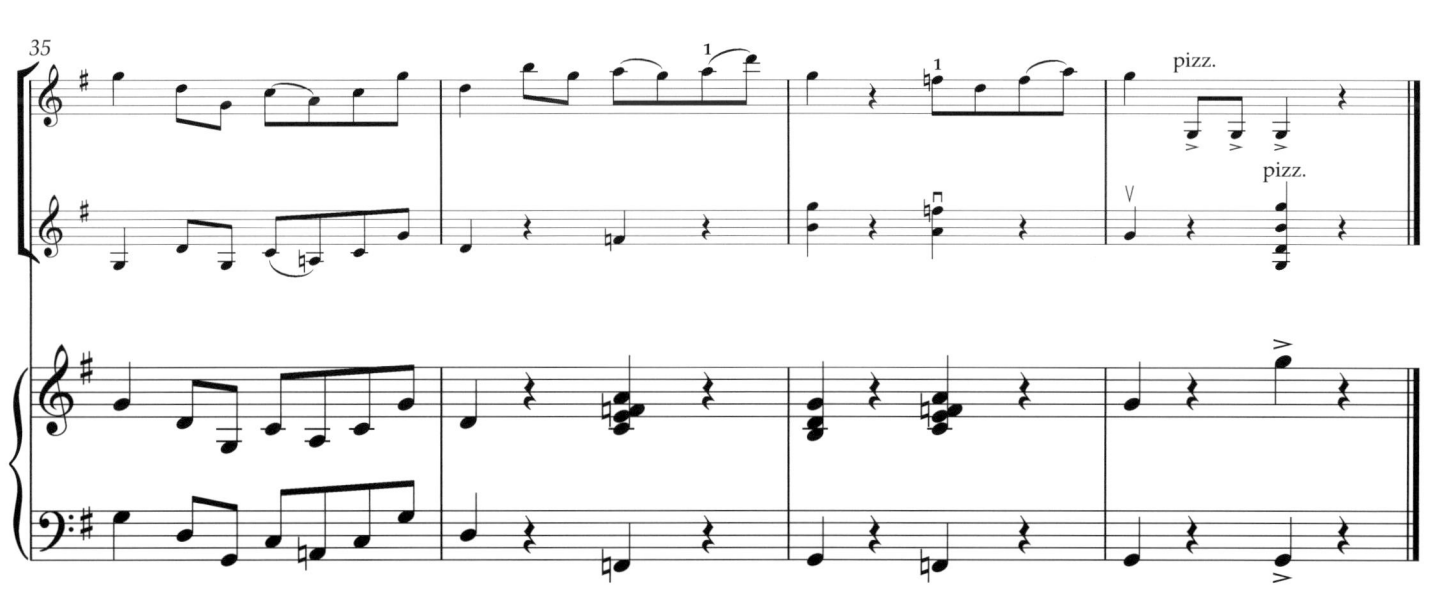

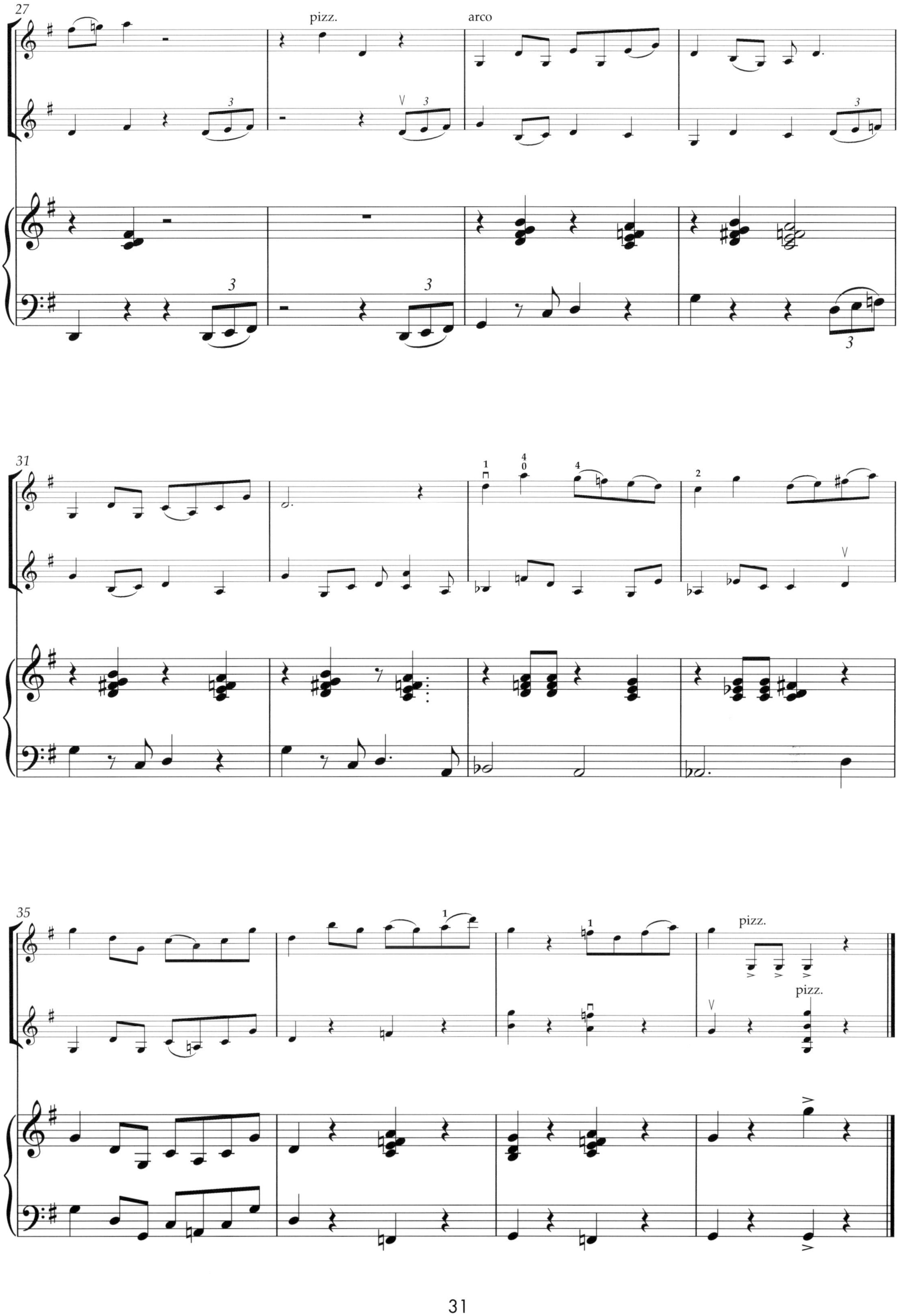
27
pizz.
arco
31
35
pizz.
pizz.

Duetto No. 2

Franz Krommer
(1759–1831)

Duo principale

Joseph Bologne,
Chevalier de Saint-Georges
(1745–1799)

Slavic March

Cécile Chaminade
(1857–1944)

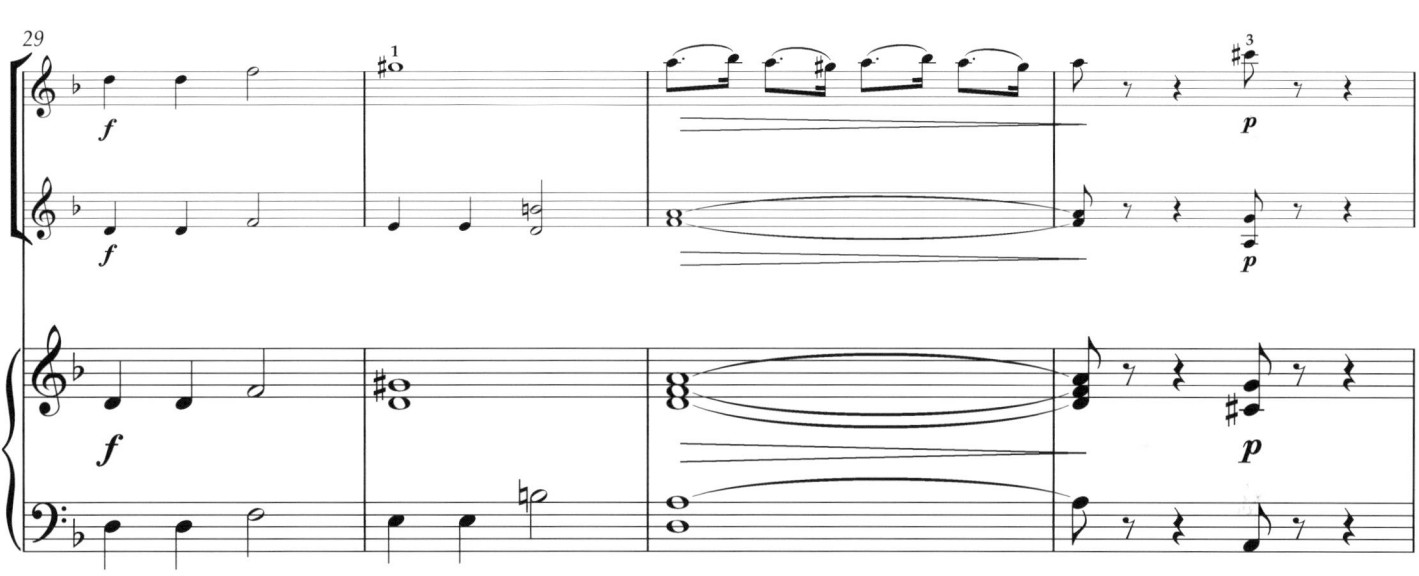

Sonata No. 4 HWV 399

George Frideric Handel
(1685–1759)

Violin solo

Gavotte

Cécile Chaminade
(1857–1944)

Violin accompaniment

Presto Op. 99 (duet part)

Joseph Haydn
(1732–1809)

Presto Op. 99

Joseph Haydn
(1732–1809)

Violin accompaniment

Yo te adoro (duet part)

Francisca Gonzaga
(1847–1935)

© 2022 by Faber Music Ltd.

Yo te adoro

Francisca Gonzaga
(1847–1935)

Violin accompaniment

Catherine the Storyteller (duet part)

Paul Harris

Violin solo

Catherine the Storyteller

Paul Harris

Duetto No. 2

Franz Krommer
(1759–1831)

Violin accompaniment

Duo principale (duet part)

Joseph Bologne,
Chevalier de Saint-Georges
(1745–1799)

© 2022 by Faber Music Ltd.

Violin solo

Duo principale

Joseph Bologne,
Chevalier de Saint-Georges
(1745–1799)

Violin accompaniment

Slavic March (duet part)

Cécile Chaminade
(1857–1944)

Violin solo

Slavic March

Cécile Chaminade
(1857–1944)

Sonata No. 4 HWV 399 (duet part)

Violin accompaniment

George Frideric Handel
(1685–1759)

Violin solo

Sonata No.4 HWV 399

George Frideric Handel
(1685–1759)